HUNKER IN MY BUNKER

When it's time to stay inside

By R. E. Lane

I will hunker in my bunker.
I will hide myself away.
I will wait inside these shadows
For a bright and clear new day.

I will paint myself some flowers
And a sky I cannot see.
I will add in all the birdies
For the joy of you and me.

I will read my favorite stories
And then write myself some more
Of the storming of a castle
And a girl who rides a boar.

I will take some food to Mama
Then to Grandpa in his bed.
I will bring a box of tissues,
And a pillow for his head.

I will wash my hands with water.
I will wash my hands with soap.
I will wash my hands so many times
But never, never mope!

I will do what Daddy tells me;
I will try to listen smart.
When we're hunkered in our bunker,
We've all got to do our part.

I will take some food to Daddy
And a tea to Mama too.
I will give her the last cookie;
It's the nicer thing to do.

I will draw a perfect map
To the gem I plan to find
In a jungle far away from here
That's deep within my mind.

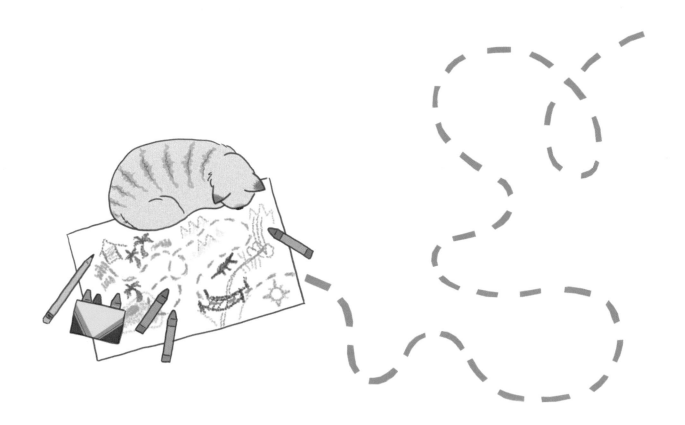

Today I'll wear pajamas
But tomorrow I'll dress up.
When you're hunkered in your bunker,
You've just got to switch it up.

I will plant a little garden;
Give it water every day.
When it grows up big and green,
I hope a fairy comes to stay.

I think I'll stay in bed today
For I'm feeling rather ill.
I will have some soup, and take a nap,
And brave that nasty pill.

I will practice all my letters.
I will try my very best,
But since my school is canceled,
There will never be a test.

I will learn to make some pancakes
With the flour that we've got,
And when we've had our fill,
I will help to clean the pot.

I will clean my room (yes, really!)
For a change of pace one day.
It doesn't hurt to rank my toys
Or have them put away.

I will hear the silly stories
That my grandpa has to tell
Of the dog that climbed a mountain
And the cow stuck in the well.

We will leave behind our bunker
When there's no more need to hide.
We will open up that door, right there;
We'll throw it open wide.

The time is coming soon, yes, soon,
When we'll see the sky above.
We'll re-emerge into the world
With all the ones we love.

Made in the USA
Monee, IL
25 May 2020